# happy

For my darling
Tydusseus
~ N.E.

For Marcus, who
makes me happy
~ K.H.

CATERPILLAR BOOKS
An imprint of the Little Tiger Group
www.littletiger.co.uk
1 Coda Studios, 189 Munster Road, London SW6 6AW
First published in Great Britain 2018
This edition published 2019
Text by Nicola Edwards • Text copyright © Caterpillar Books Ltd. 2018
Illustrations copyright © Katie Hickey 2018
A CIP Catalogue record for this book is available from the British Library
All rights reserved • Printed in China
ISBN: 978-1-84857-888-3
CPB/1800/1079/1218
2 4 6 8 10 9 7 5 3 1

# happy

Nicola Edwards

Katie Hickey

# Mindfulness

Mindfulness is all about connecting with ourselves and the world around us.

Let's take a journey together to discover some simple steps on the path to happiness.

Real life is right under our noses,

We can miss it by rushing around,

But stopping to smell life's sweet roses

Is where true

happiness

can be found.

# Listening

When we're still

there is space then to listen

To the sweet song of wind in the trees,

The gruff rumble of cars in the distance,

Or the whisper of

rustling leaves.

Take a moment to stop and really listen
to the sounds around you.

# Feeling

Even the **darkest storm** passes,

The sun can't **shine bright** every day,

We can sit with our feelings and **notice**

How they **roll through** us,

then **blow away.**

What kinds of things make you feel happy?

# Relaxing

It's not just our **minds** we get trapped in,

Our bodies can feel **tension** too,

We can **loosen** our limbs when that happens,

Like the **sun** from the **clouds**,

we **break through.**

Try tensing up all of your muscles

and then relaxing them, one by one.

# Tasting

Whether hot, salty, sweet or sour flavour,

We taste and we chew and we feel,

If we slow when we eat, we can savour

The deliciousness of every meal.

Do you notice different textures and flavours
when you chew your food slowly?

# Touching

Touch calms the wildest emotions,
We connect to the world all around,

When we dip our toes into the ocean
Or crunch crisp golden leaves on the ground.

Close your eyes and see if you can tell
what things are just by touching them.

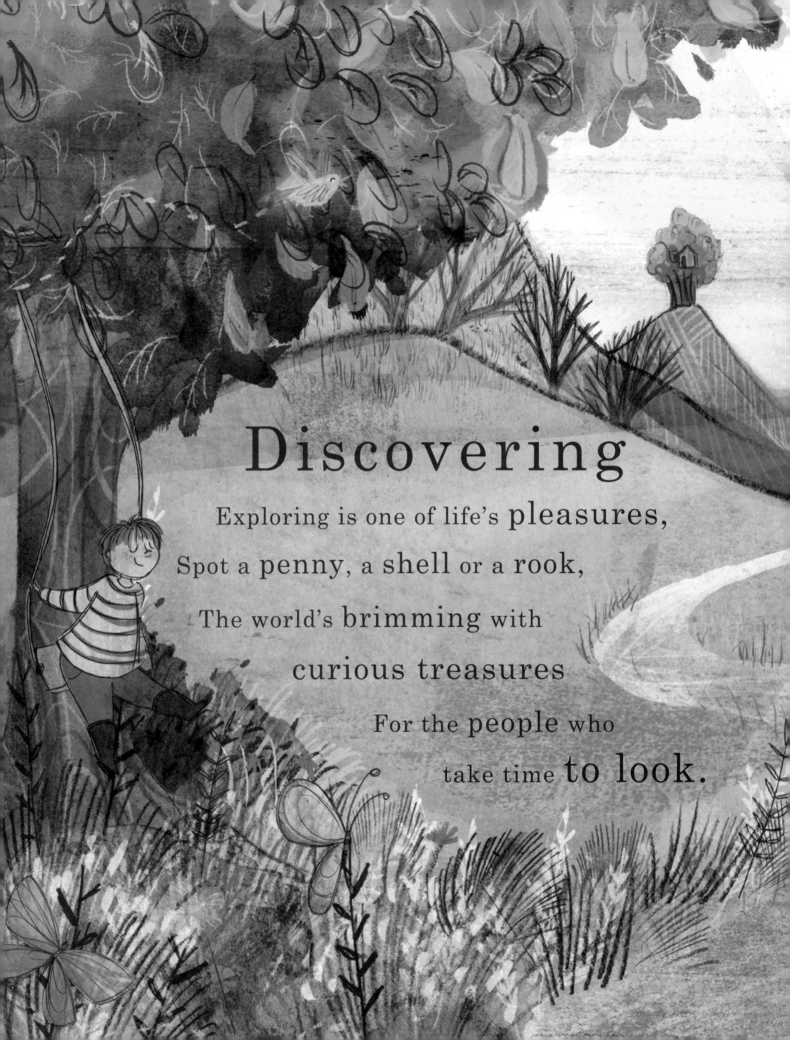

# Discovering

Exploring is one of life's pleasures,

Spot a penny, a shell or a rook,

The world's brimming with

curious treasures

For the people who

take time to look.

Look all around you
and try to spot something
you haven't noticed before.

# Smelling

When we're all tangled up in our worries,

The cool air gets us grounded again,

Wood-smoke through the sharp tang of pine trees,

Or the freshness of earth after rain.

Do the things you can smell make you feel anything or bring back any memories?

# Loving

The warmth of a hug can work wonders,

Being happy is something you feed,

With a smile or a touch or a kindness,

Even the tallest tree grows from a seed.

Have you given someone a
smile or a hug today?

# Appreciating

It feels good to give thanks at the day's end

For the pink blushing sky overhead,

A hot meal, comfy shoes or a good friend,

And the warmth of a soft cosy bed.

What good things have happened in your world today?

# Breathing

We **breathe deep** and expand like the galaxy,

We breathe out many **thousands of stars,**

And if ever we start to **feel** panicky,

This **reminds** us of just who we are.

Take a deep breath, hold it for two seconds
and then breathe out very slowly.

# Happiness

Real life is right under our noses,

It's what's here, not the future or past,

Every day is a fresh new adventure,
Now we live in the moment, at last.

How can you be more mindful each and every day?